BIONICLE®

THE Legend Reborn

BY GREG FARSHTEY

SCHOLASTIC INC.

NEW YORK   TORONTO   LONDON   AUCKLAND

SYDNEY   MEXICO CITY   NEW DELHI   HONG KONG

ISBN-13: 978-0-545-22395-9   ISBN-10: 0-545-22395-4
© 2009 The LEGO Group.

LEGO, the LEGO logo, BIONICLE, and the BIONICLE logo are trademarks of the LEGO Group. SCHOLASTIC and associated logos are trademarks and/or registered trademarks of Scholastic Inc.

12 11 10 9 8 7 6 5 4 3 2 1   10 11 12 13 14/0

Book design by Henry Ng
Printed in China 62
This edition first printing, January 2010

PROLOGUE

Through the dark void of space, a golden mask flew . . .

Seen from far away, it might have looked like a shooting star. Had someone been close enough to see what it really was, they might have wondered how such an object could have ended up among the stars. The answer would take years to tell, if one were to explore every mystery of it. But this is all the observer would truly need to know:

Once, there was a great ruler named Mata Nui. He was incredibly powerful—his body was made of metal and stood 40 million feet high. He traveled through space, exploring new worlds. His creators, known as the Great Beings, intended for him to fulfill a vital mission. But first, they wished him to learn as much as he could about the universe around him.

Unfortunately, while he focused on that universe, he ignored another one — one that existed inside his metal shell. Millions of beings lived inside of Mata Nui, and their labors gave him power. In return, he was to protect them from harm. But he grew so fascinated with the wonders of other worlds that he paid little attention to those who depended upon him.

As so often happens, neglect allows evil to breed. A conspiracy grew in Mata Nui's inner universe. Those who hungered for power struck at him, casting him into a deep sleep that lasted for a millennium. When at last he woke again, it was to find that his greatest enemy had stolen his body. Mata Nui's mind and spirit were trapped in the golden Mask of Life and hurled into space.

Now he flew through the void, out of control, knowing that his people were under the rule of a dark and unforgiving master. He had failed them. By not being vigilant, by not being wise, he had allowed himself to be forced from his body and exiled. In this new form, he had no hope of defeating his enemy.

Any other being would have surrendered to his fate. But Mata Nui knew he had a destiny to fulfill. Somehow, he vowed, he would find a way to return and free his people. It might take a thousand years, but only death would stop him from trying.

The mask's direction shifted now, as the gravitational pull of a planet took hold. It sped up, diving toward the surface, its outer skin heating up as it entered the atmosphere. The next few moments would tell the tale. Would the mask survive the heat and the impact of a crash-landing, or would it shatter, taking Mata Nui's spirit with it to destruction? Would his quest begin on the world so far below, or would it end there?

Within the golden mask, Mata Nui could do nothing now but hope. . . .

❒ O N E ❒

A swarm of scarabax beetles scurried across a sand dune, in search of their evening meal. On most evenings, this hunt was uneventful. The beetles would feed and then return to their underground tunnels. But this night was destined to be different.

One beetle lifted its eyes from the sand and saw something strange. It began clicking its pincers to alert its comrades. Other scarabax joined in, watching as a point of light streaked through the night sky and became a large fireball.

The scarabax scattered. The falling object smashed into the ground and skidded across the sands, carving out a trench as it traveled. The intense heat fused the sand to glass. Finally, it came to a halt on the edge of a dune. Smoke drifted from its metallic surface.

Slowly, the scarabax emerged from hiding. They could feel the heat coming from the object. The swarm moved closer. They didn't realize that it was a metal mask. Still, there was something about it which compelled them to draw near. . . .

Without warning, the mask rose into the air. The beetles jumped back in surprise as the sand beneath it swirled like a miniature cyclone. Now the mask hovered more than seven feet in the air, surrounded by a contained sandstorm. After a few moments, the sands began to take on a recognizable shape. Two arms, two legs, and a torso formed from the whirling grains, then turned solid.

The storm ended. There now stood a being wearing a mask. His armor was white and gold, and his body lean and strong. He brought his hands to his mask, gently, as if not certain it was real. Then he looked down at his new body.

The newcomer took a step, and his knees buckled. Catching himself, he took a deep breath before trying again. As he lifted and extended his leg, he heard a clicking sound.

Looking down, the strange being saw a scarabax beetle right where his foot was about to land. He pulled back, saying, "Sorry, little one."

The beetle moved back, cowering in fear.

"Easy," said the being. "I will not hurt you."

Responding to the stranger's gentle tone, the beetle lowered its pincers and looked up, cocking its head to one side.

"My name is Mata Nui," said the stranger. "You may have noticed I am not steady on my feet yet."

Mata Nui knelt down, extending his hand to the scarabax. The beetle sprang into his palm and scampered up his arm, clicking furiously.

"I have the feeling you're trying to tell me something," said Mata Nui. The beetle was on his shoulder now, close to his mask.

"Ah, it's the mask you're interested in."

The beetle brushed its pincer against Mata Nui's mask, making it glow brightly. For a moment, it seemed like the mask and scarabax were one. Then the glow faded, and Mata Nui could see that the insect had been transformed. Where once there had been a small beetle, there was now a full-sized shield with the symbol of a single eye in its center.

"Magnificent . . ." whispered Mata Nui in wonder.

Then the eye on the shield *blinked.*

Mata Nui jumped back, startled.

There was no time to ask questions. Mata Nui whirled at the sound of an angry hiss from above. A large, clawed creature was leaping toward him. Mata Nui tried to dodge, but he wasn't fast enough. The attacker clipped his shoulder, slamming him into the ground.

Mata Nui got a better look at his attacker. It was roughly seven feet in height, tan, with claws like spikes and a stinger tail like a scorpion. For a moment, Mata Nui wondered if this was some Toa gone mad. Then he reminded himself: *There are no Toa here! This is not your home.*

The creature attacked Mata Nui again. The shield moved to block its blows, making it angrier. Mata Nui rolled aside to avoid a strike. The beast's claws slashed deep marks in the stone where Mata Nui's head had been a moment before.

Okay, not good, thought Mata Nui. *If I stay on defense, I'll wind up in pieces.*

Mata Nui scrambled to his feet as the beast attacked again. The creature whipped its tail around, preparing to strike with its stinger. Mata Nui took a step back—and stumbled over a boulder, landing on his back in the sand. The creature hit the boulder with its stinger. The force of the impact was so strong that it shattered the rock and broke off the attacker's stinger tail. Screeching in pain, the beast ran off into the night.

Mata Nui lay on the sand and rested on his shield, trying to catch his breath.

There was a bright flash of light. "What—?"

said Mata Nui, in surprise. When the light faded, his shield was gone, returned to the form of the little scarabax beetle.

Mata Nui smiled at the insect. "Before this day, I never needed help from anyone or anything. Thank you."

He gently lowered his arm toward the ground, to allow the insect to run free. "Well, little one, I spared your life and you saved mine," he said. "Shall we call it even and go our separate ways?"

The scarabax responded with the rapid clicking of its pincers. Mata Nui chuckled, saying, "Okay, easy, it was just a—"

Mata Nui heard a sound. He turned and saw a small, white-armored figure approaching in a land vehicle. The vehicle looked like it had been patched and repaired a dozen times using pieces from wrecks. Was this another attack? Mata Nui grabbed the broken tail of the beast and stood up. The scarabax scampered up to his shoulder and hid on the back of his neck.

The driver looked at Mata Nui, then at the impact crater left by the mask, and back at Mata Nui again. He raised a crystalline sword and said, "State your business."

Mata Nui did not relax his guard. "Just a traveler looking for the nearest city," he replied.

To Mata Nui's surprise, the driver lowered his weapon and broke into a grin. "Well, then you may as well start digging," he said. "Here on Bara Magna, you're bound to find the ruins of one or another."

When Mata Nui didn't react, the driver added, "That's a joke. . . . Right. Well, to answer your question, the nearest village is Vulcanus. I've got some business there if you want a ride. That is, unless you'd rather wind up captured by a pack of Bone Hunters, or worse, Skrall."

Mata Nui didn't know this being, but he seemed friendly enough. The alternative was walking through this vast desert, with no idea which direction to go.

"What are Bone Hunters and Skrall?" asked Mata Nui.

"No one you ever want to meet."

Suddenly the driver struck at Mata Nui, who blocked the blow with the stinger tail.

"Relax!" said the driver. "You've got a filthy scarabax on your back. I was just trying to knock the disgusting thing off."

"Thanks, but I like him right where he is," answered Mata Nui, with a trace of warning in his tone.

The driver shrugged. "To each his own. I'm Metus, by the way. Now hold on!"

Metus gunned the vehicle into motion and it shot across the desert sands. They traveled for a long time through the wastelands. There was little to see—just long stretches of empty sand occasionally broken up by bizarre structures that jutted up from the ground at weird angles.

"What happened here?" Mata Nui asked finally.

"Who knows?" answered Metus. "It's

been like this as long as anyone can remember. But if I had to make a guess, I'd say it was probably—"

"Evil," said Mata Nui, softly.

Metus glanced at his passenger, then shrugged. "I was going to say 'earthquake,' maybe 'volcanic eruption,' but 'evil' works. Not from around here, are you?"

"No."

"I figured," said Metus. He pointed at the stinger tail Mata Nui carried. "It's clear you can fight if you can defeat a Vorox, and there aren't many Agori or even Glatorian who can do that."

"Agori?"

"Me. I'm an Agori," Metus said, smiling. "Although most aren't as good looking as I am. That's another joke. Truth is, we're just peaceful villagers trying to survive. Not like the Bone Hunters. They're cutthroats who steal what little we've got left."

The outline of a village appeared up ahead. Mata Nui could hear the faint sound of a crowd cheering.

"Ah, good . . . sounds like we're just in time," said Metus.

"For what?"

Metus's answer was a broad smile. He drove their vehicle into the outskirts of the village, which, to Mata Nui's surprise, seemed to be empty. From where, then, was all the cheering coming?

The answer came a moment later. The settlement was crude, built near an obviously active volcano. Light came from torches planted in the ground and red-hot magma oozed from cracks in the surface. In the center of the village was a poorly constructed arena. The citizens were clustered together, watching as two warriors — one in red armor, one in white — fought ferociously.

Metus halted the vehicle and got out. Mata Nui followed. "Back in the day, villages settled disputes the old-fashioned way — by trying to destroy one another," explained Metus. "Very messy. Lots of clean-up. So we came up with a solution. Representatives from each village fight one-on-one. . . ."

Mata Nui could hardly believe what he was seeing. In his universe, Toa fought for justice, to save lives and protect the innocent. But this was something different. "You Agori use your best warriors for . . . sport?" he asked, unable to keep the distaste out of his voice.

"Not sport—problem solving. Much more honorable than slaughtering each other. And considerably more profitable." Seeing Mata Nui's cold expression, Metus added hastily, "Errr . . . not that I care about that sort of thing."

"C'mon, Ackar! Take him down!" yelled someone in the crowd.

"Get him, Strakk!" responded another.

Metus pointed to the fighters. "The red warrior, Ackar, used to be the greatest warrior in all of Bara Magna. The white one is Strakk, from the ice village of Iconox."

An Agori, also in red armor, rose to greet Metus. "Ah, Metus. Glad you're here. Look at

Ackar. I'm telling you, his days are numbered. I practically had to beg him to fight."

"Mata Nui, meet Raanu. He's the leader of this village. Mata Nui's new in town."

Raanu nodded at Mata Nui, then returned his attention to the fight. After a few minutes, he turned to Mata Nui and said, "What do you think?"

Mata Nui gestured toward Ackar. "He fights without fear. That is a rare quality."

"True enough. But he's lost his taste for battle," said Raanu. "And once a Glatorian loses heart, it's not long before he meets defeat after defeat and must be banished. No doubt that is why Metus brought you here tonight."

"I don't understand—"

"Ha, let's not get ahead of ourselves, Raanu," Metus said, cutting off Mata Nui. "There's plenty of time to find a new First Glatorian to take Ackar's place.

In the arena, Ackar was pressing his attack. He dodged a wild swing of Strakk's ice axe and responded with a blow from his own fire sword. The impact rocked Strakk and sent his shield flying out of his hand.

"This red warrior fights with the courage of a true Toa. . . ." said Mata Nui.

Strakk swung his axe again, but once more Ackar dodged. Seeing an opening, the red-armored warrior slammed his shield into his opponent's midsection, sending Strakk flying into the arena wall. His weapon dropped from his hand as he crumpled to his knees.

The crowd exploded. "He's done it! Ackar! Ackar!"

Ackar stood over his now unarmed opponent. "Concede and this goes no further."

Strakk looked at Ackar with undisguised hatred. Then he slowly lowered his eyes, muttering, "All right. You win."

Satisfied, Ackar turned away and went to retrieve Strakk's fallen shield. "You leave with your honor intact, and I with your shield, in victory."

Behind him, Strakk grabbed his ice axe and

hurled it at Ackar's back. A shout of warning from the crowd came too late. Ackar spun and managed to catch the brunt of the blow on his shield, but the impact knocked him backward. He hit the ground, stunned.

Strakk, grinning, stalked toward Ackar and picked up his axe.

"You call this honor?" Mata Nui said to Raanu, angrily. "He was clearly defeated!"

"We're just Agori. We're not going to take on a Glatorian," Raanu replied. "The leader of his village will decide what needs to be done."

That's not good enough, thought Mata Nui. He leapt over the railing into the arena, a bright flash heralding the transformation of the scarabax into a shield once more. The sight startled the crowd. No one had ever seen a shield appear from thin air before.

"Interesting," Metus said to himself. "No wonder he's so fond of that bug. . . ."

Strakk hadn't noticed the new arrival. He was standing over the fallen Ackar, axe in hand, ready to deliver the final blow. "You're finished, old—"

Mata Nui dove, tackling Strakk. Both hit the ground, but the experienced Strakk made it to his feet first, axe at the ready.

"I'll cut you down for that, outsider!" the Glatorian growled.

Strakk struck. Mata Nui brought his shield up, but the blow knocked him right off his feet. Strakk pressed his attack, as Mata Nui desperately tried to block his strikes.

Metus shook his head. "Too bad. I'd hoped he'd bring a decent price . . ."

Mata Nui was on the ground now. Strakk stood ready to finish him off. Ackar had revived enough to see what was happening. "Your fight is with me!" Ackar shouted.

"You're next, Ackar," Strakk answered. "He asked for it, and now he's going to get it."

Mata Nui brought out the stinger tail, hoping to somehow parry the coming blow. The crude weapon touched his mask, and again, there was a bright flash of light. In the next moment, Mata Nui no longer wielded a broken stinger, but a bright, gleaming sword.

The crowd gasped and Metus's eyes widened in shock. Strakk staggered back. "How in —?"

Mata Nui seized the moment. He lashed out with a sweeping kick that brought Strakk down and caused him to lose his grip on the ice axe. Mata Nui leapt to his feet, holding the blade of his new weapon at Strakk's throat.

"Concede," said Mata Nui coldly.

"Fine . . ." Strakk growled.

"For all to hear!" snapped Mata Nui.

Strakk glared at Mata Nui for a moment before shouting, "I concede!"

The crowd went wild, their cheers shaking the arena. Ackar walked unsteadily to Mata Nui's side. Spotting Strakk's hand inching toward his axe, Ackar stepped on the weapon, saying, "Don't." The ice Glatorian rose and limped out of the arena.

"What will happen to him?" asked Mata Nui.

"For attacking after he conceded?

Banishment. Iconox can't afford to send Glatorian without honor into the arena. Strakk will be reduced to living in the wastelands before the week is out." Ackar offered Mata Nui the ice warrior's shield.

Mata Nui shook his head. "You won honorably. The prize of victory is yours."

"In that case . . ." Ackar tossed the shield aside as if it were garbage. "I've got plenty of shields."

Ackar turned to look at the crowd. Most of the Agori were already filing out of the arena, not even looking in his direction. "How quickly they forget," he said softly. "I am already an outcast."

"It's never too late to win them back," answered Mata Nui.

Ackar shrugged. "Perhaps. . . . I am in your debt, stranger."

Mata Nui said nothing. But he wondered if he had just found the most valuable treasure that might exist on this world: an ally.

⊃⊂ TWO ⊂⊃

Mata Nui followed Ackar to his shelter in the village. The Glatorian began packing items into a satchel, explaining that he was due to fight another match in the village of Tesara.

The walls of the shelter were lined with Glatorian shields, trophies of Ackar's past victories. "You won all these?" asked Mata Nui.

"Yes. And look what good they do me," Ackar answered, making no attempt to hide his bitterness. "Should have packed it in long ago."

"But you stayed. Why?"

Ackar paused a moment before answering. When he spoke again, he sounded less bitter than sad. "Duty. Pride. But a Glatorian past his prime's no good to anyone."

"To be defeated without a fight would be

dishonor. You carry this truth inside you, as do I. You are a true Toa," said Mata Nui.

"Toa?"

"Where I come from . . ." Mata Nui began. Then he stopped, as if not sure how to explain himself. Finally, he said, "It is a name given to a select few warriors, worthy of —"

Metus burst into the shelter, practically leaping in the air with excitement. "Mata Nui! You were brilliant! Raanu will pay anything we ask. And if you don't like this village — no problem! I'll get the other leaders to bid for you."

"That is very kind," said Mata Nui. "But . . . no."

Metus looked at Mata Nui as if he had just said he wanted to be a target dummy for the Skrall. "Are you crazy? Do you realize what you're passing up? The life of a First Glatorian!"

"Yes, just look how great it worked out for me," Ackar muttered.

"The answer is still no."

"Okay, okay, I hear you. But when you change your mind—"

Mata Nui held firm. "I will not."

"Playing hard to get, eh? I can respect that. Soon enough, you'll come around, begging me to take you back."

Mata Nui took a step toward Metus, obviously not amused by the suggestion. Metus took a step back.

"Okay, that's a joke. You'd never beg. Heh, heh . . . I'm going now." Metus turned and rushed out of the shelter. Ackar laughed at the sight, and after a moment, Mata Nui joined him.

"So, stranger, what are your plans?" asked Ackar.

"I must begin searching for a way back to my homeland."

"Which is . . . ?"

"You will think it sounds crazy . . ."

"No crazier than jumping into an arena armed with only a stinger tail and that thing,"

Ackar said, gesturing toward the scarabax perched on Mata Nui's shoulder.

"True. My home is far from this place . . . on another world entirely," said Mata Nui. "I was once its protector, until I lost everything to a powerful evil that has enslaved my people. That is why I must find a way back."

A blue-armored Glatorian suddenly sprang from the shadows near the door, startling them both. "I knew it! Woo-hoo! Proof! Proof of what I've been saying for years!" shouted the newcomer.

"Kiina—!? What are you—!?" Ackar snapped. "This is not the place!"

Their visitor was female. She was tall and wiry, and looked as if she would be a formidable foe in a fight. Right now, though, she was either extremely happy or completely insane; Mata Nui wasn't sure which. And he wasn't in the mood to take chances. Mata Nui went for his weapon.

"Just who is this?"

Ackar reached out to restrain Mata Nui. "Wait, she's—"

The female Glatorian came right up close to Mata Nui. "Name's Kiina. A Glatorian. One of the best. And you just won me a lot of bets." She turned to Ackar. "'Kiina's delusional. There's no such thing as other worlds.' Yeah, well, he proves there are!"

Ackar gently guided Mata Nui's arm down, so that his sword was pointed at the floor. "It's okay. Although I don't always agree with her methods—such as lurking in the shadows—as Glatorian go, Kiina ranks. I'd trust her with my life . . . and have, more than once."

Mata Nui looked from Ackar to Kiina. He still thought she was unbalanced, but if she was a friend of Ackar's . . . well, he had to take his allies where he could find them now. "Good to meet you, Kiina," he said.

The scarabax on his shoulder clicked its approval. Kiina looked at the insect with undisguised revulsion. "So what they're saying is true?" she asked Ackar.

Ackar nodded.

She turned back to Mata Nui. "Let me guess. You call him 'Click'," she said, more than a little sarcasm in her voice.

The scarabax, as if sensing her contempt, lashed out with a pincer and clicked angrily. She took a step back. "Hey, I was just kidding."

Mata Nui smiled. "Actually, I like it. Click it is."

Kiina walked in a wide circle around Mata Nui, checking him out from every angle. She had always dreamed of meeting someone from another planet. Somehow, though, she had thought they would look less like the other Glatorian she knew. It was an exciting moment just the same.

"Wow—a real other-worlder," she said. "Finally, someone to convince the Agori there's a better place than this miserable wasteland."

Ackar frowned. He considered Kiina a good friend, but he also knew she could be selfish. He didn't want to see Mata Nui used. "He needs our help, Kiina. I owe him," he said.

Kiina looked right at Mata Nui. "Help, huh? I might be able to do something for you. But I'm going to want something in return." She moved closer, her helmet practically touching Mata Nui's mask. "I want out of this dump. You have to take me with you."

"Kiina . . ." said Ackar, shaking his head.

"It's all right," said Mata Nui. He studied Kiina for a moment, then said, "If it's within my power, I will take you. But the time to help my people is running out."

"No problem," Kiina said, smiling. "I work fast."

"What do you have in mind, Kiina?" asked Ackar. He didn't know of any way to get off Bara Magna.

"Well, I discovered an enormous cavern under my village. It's filled with weird, ancient equipment and tools. It might have something you can use. Word of warning, though . . ." She pointed an armored finger at Mata Nui.

"Don't even think of pulling a fast one—'cause you're my ticket out of here."

Whose bright idea was this again? Kiina asked herself. She, Ackar, and Mata Nui were in a borrowed dune chariot, on their way to the water village of Tajun. It was dawn.

Traveling in daylight was not Kiina's idea of a good time. It didn't take long for the temperature to soar in the desert of Bara Magna. If the vehicle kept running, they would make it to the village before high sun. But dune chariots were notoriously unreliable—and this one looked to be patched and repaired a dozen times over. She would have been happier riding her sand stalker, but the animal was ill.

Heat wasn't the only worry. There was no cover out in the middle of the trackless wastes. Granted, the savage Vorox would be more likely to hunt at night, but in full sunshine, Bone Hunters could see potential victims coming a mile away.

Of course, there is some good news, thought Kiina. *You can see them, too.*

Mata Nui pointed toward a canyon up ahead. "Is the cavern in that canyon?"

Kiina shook her head. "No. It's near Tajun, my village, just beyond that canyon."

Ackar wasn't listening. His eyes were scanning the horizon, looking for threats. It had not been that long ago that Bone Hunters had attacked Vulcanus, and Skrall had sacked the free city of Atero. No place on Bara Magna was safe, least of all the wastelands between villages.

Had he been able to see what was going on behind him, Ackar would have been even more worried. Shortly after their departure from Vulcanus, an Agori slipped out of the village. Making his way up into the rocks, he ran into two Bone Hunters on their rock steeds.

Bone Hunters were an unusual breed. Distantly related to the rock tribe of Roxtus, they were nomadic bandits. They lived in the desert, surviving on stew made from the Thornax plant—and whatever they could steal. They were excellent trackers and unafraid to go after prey even in the worst heat of the day. Normally, they robbed and killed their victims. Lately, they had begun kidnapping Glatorian, for reasons unknown.

Under ordinary circumstances, an Agori who encountered a Bone Hunter would scream and run. But these weren't ordinary circumstances, and this Agori was right where he had planned to be.

"The Glatorian are heading for Tajun," he told the two riders. "You know what to do."

The two Bone Hunters glanced at each other. They weren't used to taking orders from villagers. Agori were for robbing, after all. But it had been made clear to them that this Agori's word was to be obeyed. So they grunted something close to a "yes" and rode off.

The Agori watched them go. He didn't trust the Bone Hunters—what sane being would?—but he needed them. Left on their own, they were a dangerous element, unpredictable and wild. But bribed with weapons and water, they could be "tamed" and used. And once they were no longer useful . . .

He smiled, then, a little smile with no cheer in it. Then he turned back to Vulcanus. He couldn't let his absence be noticed by anyone, not when he was so close to achieving his goals. So it was time to go back to playing the role of trusted Agori: a little eccentric, maybe, but all in all, a good being to have around. And all the while, he would be laughing inside at the thought of what waited for the fools of the fire village.

"I don't like this," said Ackar. "It's the perfect place for an ambush."

The dune chariot had reached the mouth of the canyon. Places like this made the red-armored Glatorian wary. It hadn't been that long ago that he had helped set up an intricate series of traps in Iron Canyon for a Bone Hunter raiding party. All the skill of the bandits had not helped them at all in a place where they were stuck on a narrow path, being picked off by Glatorian hidden among the rocks above.

"Please," said Kiina. "Even Bone Hunters aren't stupid enough to take on three Glatorian."

This, of course, was a lie, and she knew it. With the element of surprise on their side, Bone Hunters would try almost anything. But she didn't want Mata Nui to get nervous and decide he wanted off this ride.

Ackar knew exactly what she was doing, and he wasn't planning to let her get away with it. He owed Mata Nui. If they were going to expose him to danger, he had a right to know what kind and how nasty things were likely to get.

"They're getting bolder," he said to Kiina. There was an edge in his voice that said, *Watch it, I'm on to you.* "Skrall, too. In the past few months, they've seemed to know our every move before we make it."

"True," Kiina conceded. "But don't worry. It's not like we've got much worth stealing. Well . . . maybe Mata Nui does."

The scarabax beetle sitting on Mata Nui's shoulder clicked its pincers in enthusiastic agreement.

"I was talking about his blade, bug face," Kiina snapped at the beetle, and shook her head. "I can't believe I'm talking to an insect."

Mata Nui did not crack a smile. "In my experience, when an enemy knows too much, it can only mean one thing: You have a traitor on your hands."

Ackar nodded. "I was thinking the same thing. But who?"

A low rumbling sound filled the air. The ground beneath the chariot began to shake violently. Then the rumbling became a roar as, up ahead, the earth buckled and heaved.

"I think we have a bigger problem!" Kiina yelled.

The ground exploded. A massive crimson creature rose up on four great legs and let out an earsplitting roar. Mata Nui had never seen anything like it. It was at least forty feet tall, part animal and part machine. Its legs sported massive treads and ended in vicious claws. Sharp pincers extended from both sides of its jagged mouth. When it took a step, the earth shook — and the chariot was headed straight for it.

"Skopio!" shouted Ackar. He had seen this creature once before, from a distance. Getting this close to one was something he could have lived without.

"We should turn back," said Mata Nui.

"Can't," Ackar said, pointing behind the chariot. "They're even deadlier."

Mata Nui turned. A group of black-armored riders mounted on reptilian creatures were riding across the sands in pursuit of the chariot. Each held a sword aloft in the air and shouted war cries as they rode.

"What are they?" asked Mata Nui.

"Bone Hunters," Ackar answered, "and a lot of them."

"My village—there's another Glatorian there," said Kiina, leaning forward in the driver's seat. "We just have to make it there!"

Kiina turned the wheel and aimed the chariot at the narrow gap between the Skopio's left foreleg and the canyon wall. The creature's eyes narrowed and it whipped its leg to the side, blocking the vehicle. Kiina yanked on the wheel, sending the chariot into a skid right in front of the beast.

"Hang on tight!" yelled Kiina.

The Skopio slammed its right foreleg into the sand, missing the chariot by centimeters. Kiina drove it up the side of the canyon wall. The beast swung again—and missed. Kiina vaulted the chariot off the wall and over a dune. But she wasn't quite fast enough. The Skopio landed a glancing blow, sending the chariot tumbling end over end and hurling the three occupants onto the sand.

Ackar and Mata Nui rolled to their feet, weapons drawn, facing the oncoming Bone Hunters. "Help Kiina," Mata Nui said to Ackar. "I'll draw the beast away from you."

"Good luck," said Ackar, dropping into a crouch to await the first attacker.

Mata Nui glanced down at Click. "Are you ready?"

The beetle snapped its pincers together in response. Then there was a bright flash as it transformed once more into a mighty shield. Mata Nui charged toward the Skopio.

Behind him, Ackar and Kiina were both locked in battle. Kiina parried a Bone Hunter's sword with her staff, looking for an opening. When she saw the Hunter drop his guard, she struck, landing a solid blow with her weapon and hurling him from his rock steed. Two more Bone Hunters closed in. Kiina moved like quicksilver, keeping her enemies off-balance with sweeping kicks.

Nearby, Ackar was surrounded, fierce but outnumbered. *Fighting mounted warriors on foot is a losing game*, he thought. *So it's time to even the odds a little.*

A Bone Hunter rode down on him, sword flashing in the sunlight. Ackar blocked the Hunter's blade with his own. As the Bone Hunter drew back to strike again, Ackar launched himself into the air and landed a solid kick, knocking the Bone Hunter out of the saddle. The Glatorian landed atop the rock steed and urged it forward.

Up ahead, Kiina was hard-pressed in a fight against a bigger, stronger Bone Hunter. Ackar rode toward her, battling the Hunters on either side of him. As soon as he drew close to the canyon wall, he hurled himself from the saddle, somersaulting in the air — once, twice, three times. He came out of the move feetfirst, slamming into Kiina's opponent and knocking him senseless. Now Kiina and Ackar stood back to back as the Bone Hunters closed in.

Mata Nui was having problems of his own with the Skopio. Its attention was now fully focused on him, which was what he wanted. Its blows were coming dangerously close to landing, though, and Mata Nui had learned at least this about his new body: It grew tired. And if he slowed down even a step, the Skopio would finish him.

The great beast, meanwhile, was growing impatient. It was time to crush this golden-armored pest. The Skopio concentrated, triggering the mechanical Thornax launcher built into it ages ago. With a hiss of hydraulics and a metallic hum, the launcher rose from the creature's back and locked into place. Taking aim at Mata Nui, the Skopio fired.

Mata Nui stopped dead. For just a moment, he watched the beast's transformation in disbelief. That delay almost cost him his life, as he barely got his shield up in time to take the brunt of the blast. Even with its protection, he was still knocked off his feet. The Skopio advanced, lifting a clawed leg into the air, ready to crush him. Mata Nui rolled to dodge the blow, landing neatly in a crouch. This time, he'd be ready for the Skopio's next attack.

Behind him, he heard the sound of Kiina's voice. "Ackar!" she said. "We're finished unless we can make it to my village."

"Try and get to the chariot," Mata Nui yelled to the two Glatorian. "I have an idea."

When the Skopio swung a leg at him again, Mata Nui didn't try to move aside. Instead, he launched into the air and grabbed onto the leg. As the Skopio drew its limb back, Mata Nui was pulled high into the air. When he was at the same level as the monster's head, Mata Nui jumped off the leg and landed on the Skopio's back.

It took Mata Nui only a moment to figure out the controls for the mounted Thornax launcher. Aiming at the Bone Hunters menacing Ackar and Kiina, he fired. The blast scattered the Hunters like grains of sand before a fierce wind. Ackar and Kiina took advantage of the opening to run for the chariot. Bone Hunters who pursued them were met by another devastating Thornax blast, courtesy of Mata Nui.

Angered by its unwanted rider, the Skopio whipped its stinger tail forward, knocking Mata Nui off his perch. He twisted in midair and managed to land on his feet on a high ledge. Down below, Ackar and Kiina had reached the vehicle and were speeding toward the Skopio, hoping to slip underneath the creature. Mounted Bone Hunters galloped close behind.

Mata Nui drew his sword and plunged it into the rock beneath his feet. The power of the blade split the stone, sending half of it tumbling down the mountainside. It struck other boulders, knocking them loose. Soon, the whole mountainside seemed to be moving, stones careening down in a huge rockslide.

Kiina heard the sound of the avalanche

and saw the first rocks strike the sand up ahead. "This is going to be close!" she yelled to Ackar, pushing the chariot to full speed. The metal frame of the vehicle shook violently, bolts snapping off and flying in every direction.

Spotting a gap barely large enough for the chariot, Kiina aimed right for it. The vehicle shot through it and onto open sand just as the rain of rock brought the Skopio down with a tremendous crash. The Bone Hunters weren't so lucky—they were under the creature as it fell, buried beneath its body and a ton of rock.

As they neared the mouth of the canyon, Kiina allowed herself a relieved sigh. Then she suddenly realized someone was missing. "Hey, where—?"

Ackar pointed off to the east. "There!"

Kiina saw him now, too. Mata Nui was surfing down the side of the mountain on his shield, vaulting over outcroppings as if he had been doing it all his life. One particularly large rock sent him high into the air. He somer-saulted, grabbing his shield and spinning into an upright position just in time to land on the hood of the chariot.

Ackar laughed. "Gutsiest move I've ever seen."

"Woo-hoo! Those Bone Hunters are going to be eating Skopio belly for weeks," Kiina said, smiling broadly. "Not bad, other-worlder."

Ackar's grin abruptly vanished from his face. He laid a hand on Kiina's arm, as if to steady her against a shock. She glanced at him, then up ahead—and that's when she saw it.

A plume of black smoke rose from the nearby oasis. Flames shot through the cloud of ash and soot. As they drew nearer, Kiina could hear the sound of shelters collapsing, sand stalkers screeching in fear and pain, and something even more chilling: the war cries of Skrall.

Tajun was burning.

⊃⊂ T H R E E ⊃⊂

By the time the trio reached the village, it was too late. The once-proud village of Tajun was a pile of ashes, or soon would be. Kiina stood in the middle of the chaos, looking around desperately, stricken with grief.

"Looks like the Agori got away," said Ackar. "A daylight raid . . . one of their sentries must have spotted the attackers in time."

"The village . . . our homes . . . this is my fault! I should have been here to help. Where's Tarix? And Gresh? We had a training session scheduled for today. He's just a rookie. He wouldn't be prepared for—"

Gresh was a young Glatorian from the jungle village of Tesara. Although new to the sport, he was highly skilled and had been fast gaining a reputation as a potential champion. But not even a veteran

Glatorian could win against a Skrall war party.

"There!" yelled Ackar, pointing to the western side of the village.

Gresh staggered out of the smoke, clutching his shoulder. His armor was battered and one arm hung limply at his side.

"He's hurt!" said Kiina. She, Ackar, and Mata Nui rushed to his side.

"Easy, son," said Ackar, reaching out to support him.

Gresh pushed them away. "I'm fine. I'll be fine," he said, his voice weak. Then his face contorted and he grabbed at his injured shoulder. His knees buckled and only fast action by Ackar and Mata Nui kept him from collapsing.

"Just shut up and let us help you," growled Ackar.

"We need to get him out of sight," said Mata Nui. "Kiina, your cavern—"

"Right," said Kiina. "The entrance is this way."

The party made its way through the thick smoke, moving as quickly as they could with the injured Gresh in tow. The young Glatorian, gasping for breath, was still trying to talk.

"Stay quiet," said Mata Nui. "You will be safe soon."

"No," Gresh answered. "You don't understand. . . . Skrall and Bone Hunters . . . they're working together."

"Impossible," replied Ackar. "They're rival tribes. Neither allies with anyone, least of all each other."

Gresh grabbed Ackar's arm. "No! I watched them destroy our village. . . . I . . ." His eyes went wide for an instant, then suddenly closed. He sagged in Ackar's arms.

"Gresh!" said Kiina. "He isn't . . . ?"

"Still alive," Ackar reassured her.

"But not for long, if that savage sees us," Mata Nui said.

The others turned at his words. Moving through the smoke was a giant of a being, a warrior clad in black-and-green armor and carrying a huge sword. Kiina had seen him only once before, but it was impossible to forget the sight.

"Tuma," she breathed. "Leader of the Skrall."

Now more figures appeared behind him, a combination of Skrall warriors on foot and mounted Bone Hunters. Kiina felt sick. This was every Agori's worst nightmare, coming true before her eyes.

"The boy was telling the truth," said Ackar quietly. "The Bone Hunters have joined forces with the Skrall."

Kiina pushed on a jutting piece of stone and a portion of the rock wall slid open. The group rushed inside and the door slid in place behind them. "They won't find us in here."

She led her friends down a gently sloping tunnel. The stone walls were marked with strange glyphs and symbols, carved with care. Mata Nui found he could not take his eyes off them, despite the danger that surrounded him.

"Wait," he said. "These glyphs . . . I . . ."

"Later," snapped Kiina. "First we have to take care of Gresh. The cavern is just ahead."

The tunnel opened onto a massive cave. This was no natural formation. Huge, opaque, marble obelisks dominated the center of the space, illuminating a central area. Six entrances opened onto what looked like miniature ecosystems.

It looks like a . . . place of creation, thought Mata Nui. *A lab, perhaps? But why create six environments in this place? For what purpose? If it was a test . . . what were they testing?*

As they moved farther in, Mata Nui saw more evidence for his theory. Tables made of stone were scattered about, covered with tools and machine parts. Someone had been working here and perhaps not so long ago — he noted disturbances in the ancient dust.

Kiina gestured to one of the tables. "Lay him down over here."

Gresh's breathing was steady, but one arm

was badly injured. Mata Nui felt helpless. He knew nothing about how to care for another being. He wasn't even certain how serious the damage to Gresh might be—would he die from this wound? Or was this the kind of injury Glatorian received in the arena all the time? He guessed not, given how worried Kiina appeared to be.

The keen ears of Ackar picked up a sound from the shadows. He drew his sword in a flash, saying, "Show yourself. Now!"

There was a long moment of stillness and silence. Then a villager clad in blue armor stepped into the light. He was short and his body seemed to be in constant nervous motion. He held his hands out defensively, looking from Ackar to Kiina and back again.

"Okay, okay, relax," the Agori villager said. "Everything's okay. It's just me—Berix."

Now Kiina had her trident in hand, pointing it toward Berix. Her features were tight with anger. "You filthy little thief! I told you if

I ever caught you down here again, I'd—"

Berix ducked behind Mata Nui's legs. "This place doesn't belong to you. And I'm no thief—I'm a collector." He glanced up at Mata Nui then, noticing his "protector" for the first time. "Ooh . . . like your mask. Can I have it?"

The villager reached up to touch the Mask of Life. But before his fingers could make contact, Berix spotted Kiina rushing toward him. He withdrew his hand quickly, as if the mask might bite him.

"Come here, you!" snapped Kiina.

Berix sidestepped, keeping Mata Nui between him and the enraged Glatorian. "I have a right to collect anything I want. It's just junk anyway."

"Then why do you want it?" asked Kiina.

"'Cause I like fixing things," said Berix. He gestured at the lights on the ceiling. "Who do you think got those lights working?"

"I was wondering about that. . . ." Kiina grumbled.

Berix looked up at Mata Nui again. Spotting the scarabax perched on the warrior's shoulder, he took a step back. "Hey, you've got a—"

"He knows!" Kiina and Ackar said in unison.

There was too much anger in this chamber, Mata Nui decided. It wasn't helping Gresh or anyone else. "Berix, have you ever fixed an injured Glatorian?"

"Oh, no," Kiina said immediately. "No way. He's not touching Gresh."

"The boy needs help, Kiina," Ackar said quietly.

Kiina started to say something, then stopped. Slowly, the tension left her body. Ackar was right, she knew. Gresh was injured badly—she would not be able to help him on her own.

Berix gestured to his own battered armor. "Well, I've had to patch myself up a few times."

"Right," said Kiina. "Like every time you've been pounded on for stealing."

Berix moved to the table to take a look at Gresh, but couldn't resist snapping back, "*Collecting.* Maybe you should let me work on your ears next, Kiina."

"Enough," Mata Nui said. "Can you fix him?"

Berix shrugged. "Yeah. Okay, yeah . . . I think I can."

The Agori tapped his arm. A small panel opened in his armor. Inside was a compartment stuffed with various tools, wires, and odds and ends. He reached inside and took out a crude knife.

"Gresh better pull through," Kiina said. "You got that?"

"Great," Berix muttered. "No pressure or anything." He took the knife and sliced off a portion of a strange vine that grew on the nearby wall.

Ackar took Kiina's arm gently and led her a few steps away from the table. She never took her eyes off of Berix, watching him with the look of a mother sand stalker ready to spring to the defense of its young. "What if he's the traitor?" she whispered.

"Then he'll pay," Ackar replied.

The two Glatorian moved to join Mata Nui, who was examining the cavern with undisguised curiosity. He moved hesitantly, as if he were trying to capture a memory that was just out of reach.

"Something wrong?" asked Kiina.

"I don't know," Mata Nui answered. "There's a familiarity about this place."

"Must have been created by the old rulers of Bara Magna," said Ackar, looking around.

"The Great Beings," nodded Kiina.

Mata Nui's head snapped around at the sound of the name. "The Great Beings were here?"

It was too incredible to believe. The Great Beings were at the core of Mata Nui's earliest recollections. They had constructed the massive robot body that had once belonged to him. They had created his consciousness and placed it inside that body, and then sent him forth to do . . . what? He still did not recall. That had been more than 100,000 years ago and he had given up hoping he would ever find them again. It might have been chance that brought him to this world, where the Great Beings had once walked, but he preferred to think it was destiny.

It was obvious that Kiina did not share Mata Nui's reverence for the Great Beings, though. "Great Destroyers is more like it," she said.

"Why do you speak against them?" demanded Mata Nui.

"Why? They wrecked our world, that's why," Kiina shot back. Gesturing toward the six chambers containing mini-environments, she continued, "This was Bara Magna before the Great Beings left us here to rot."

"You have no proof of that, Kiina," said Ackar. "They could have just as easily ended up buried in the ruins. A lot of others did, you know."

"No," Mata Nui said, shaking his head. "The

Great Beings did not fall here. That much I am sure of."

He walked deeper into the cave, examining every inch of the walls, until he came to a great door. Inscribed on it was a symbol—three dots flanked by two curved lines. Mata Nui had seen the symbol before, for it had been inscribed in places on his old robotic body as well. But he did not know what it stood for.

"What lies beyond here?" he asked.

"No idea," Kiina replied. "Never been able to get it open."

Berix had been eavesdropping on the conversation as he worked. Now he called over his shoulder, "Me, neither! But I bet there's something good back there."

"Keep dreaming," Kiina said sharply. "And pay attention to what you're doing, thief."

Mata Nui stepped close to the door. As he did so, his mask began to glow, casting golden light on the inscribed image. "I recognize this symbol," he said softly.

He reached out and touched one of the three dots. As soon as he did so, it began to glow, and there was a loud click, as if a lock was coming undone. The symbol rotated beneath Mata Nui's hand, and the two halves of the door began to slide apart.

"It's opening," said Kiina. "You did it!"

Behind the door there was a stone staircase leading down. Mata Nui and the two Glatorian followed it into an antechamber farther beneath the earth. A variety of symbols covered the walls, most of them circles with lines or other circles inside of them. Kiina and Ackar examined these as Mata Nui moved farther into the chamber. Then they heard him cry out, "It cannot be!"

Ackar and Kiina were at his side instantly. He was standing in front of the far wall. Carved into the wall were what looked like building plans for a giant being made of metal. It was clear from the dust all around that the carving had been made long, long ago.

"What's wrong? You look like you've seen a ghost," said Kiina.

"I have," replied Mata Nui, his eyes riveted by the carving.

"You know that thing?"

"Yes. A gigantic mechanical being," Mata Nui said, his tone filled with frustration and anger. "Just like the one now enslaving my people."

"Wait," said Kiina. "You think the Great Beings had something to do with that? Did they harm your people, too?"

"No. The responsibility lies on my shoulders alone," said Mata Nui. "But this place . . . these symbols . . . we are on the right track."

⊃⊂ F O U R ⊃⊂

Tuma, leader of the Skrall, was feeling quite satisfied.

He had returned to the city of Roxtus following the sack of Tajun, confident that his plans were proceeding. With that village and its oasis in his hands, the Agori of Bara Magna had lost their primary water source. No doubt they would turn on each other now in a fight over what water remained in the wastelands, making them easy pickings for his Skrall warriors. In one swift stroke, he would control the desert.

To an outsider, it might have seemed a strange prize to covet. After all, what was there to Bara Magna? Nothing but scattered metallic shelters that towered hundreds of feet high, with Agori huddled inside them for protection against the wind and sand;

deposits of exsidian metal and other semi-valuable minerals here and there; precious little food or water . . . on the face of it, nothing a conqueror like Tuma would want.

But the desert of Bara Magna offered one thing the Skrall desperately needed: space. No one other than the Skrall knew why they had first moved down from the north into the Black Spike Mountains. Their cities had been raided and destroyed by a race of warriors they had never encountered before, shape-shifters who struck from the shadows and then disappeared. All of the Skrall's weapons and skill had proven of no use against this enemy. Finally, the Skrall were forced south, taking up residence in the long-abandoned city that became Roxtus.

Here, they were easily the most powerful tribe. But Tuma could not help looking behind. Would their enemies from the north follow them here? If so, how would the Skrall stop them? Fighting the shapeshifters in confined quarters would lead to a second disaster. The

Skrall needed room to maneuver, vast tracts of open land they could force the foe to cross. Only then would they have a fighting chance to survive.

Tuma could have simply warned the Agori of Bara Magna of what the Skrall had encountered and made some mutual defense agreement with the other villages. But that was not the Skrall way of doing things. No, instead he plotted, manipulated, and steadily weakened the villages until he was sure they could not stand against his army. Then the Skrall struck at the village of Atero, destroying it, and now Tajun had fallen as well. Complete surrender by the Agori would follow any day now.

Then Tuma would rule not just a city, but an empire . . . and it would be an empire he would keep, no matter who might dare to attack it.

A pair of Bone Hunters stood guard amid the ruins of Tajun. They were not happy. Their role in life was to ride, hunt, rob, and kill. It was the nature of their people to take from those who were weaker. Bone Hunters saw themselves as akin to the cruel wind that blew out of the Black Spike Mountains, raising sandstorms that blinded and killed those foolish enough to be caught out in the desert. Through their hunts, they eliminated those Glatorian and Agori who were not fit to survive.

That had changed since the alliance with the Skrall. Now they had to take orders from Tuma and his lieutenants, even if doing so meant standing around and watching over a pile of ashes.

As it turned out, the Bone Hunters were right: They were not made for guard duty. If they had been, they might have heard Ackar before he sprang up behind them and knocked their heads together. Instead, both slumped to the ground, unconscious.

Kiina appeared behind Ackar. "You have all the fun," she chided him. "I get the next two."

Ackar didn't smile. "Let's move. We need to warn the villages about the Skrall and Bone Hunters uniting."

Kiina nodded. "And that we have a traitor on the inside."

Mata Nui and Berix emerged from the cave, supporting Gresh between them. The young Glatorian had his arm in a makeshift sling of vine.

"How are you holding up?" Mata Nui asked Gresh.

"I'm fine," said the wounded Glatorian. "You don't need to baby me. But I could use a new weapon. The Skrall shredded my shield."

Ackar and Kiina both looked at their own weapons, each heavily damaged by the recent battle with the Bone Hunters. "Get in line," said Kiina.

Berix reached for Kiina's trident. "I might be able to—"

Kiina yanked it away. "Don't even think about it."

"Wait," said Ackar. He turned to Mata Nui. "What you did with the Vorox stinger, and Click. Could it work with my sword and her trident?"

Mata Nui reached up and touched the metal surface of his mask. "I don't know. This mask . . . gave me new life. But I still don't completely understand its power. I am certain it only works on things that are, or were, alive . . . like the stinger."

"No problem," said Berix. "Most Glatorian weapons have bone or claw cores."

"'Collected' a few, have you?" said Kiina.

Mata Nui took Ackar's sword in hand. "It's worth a try, anyway."

The others watched as he raised the sword to his brow. "Together . . . as one mind," Mata Nui said, so softly they could barely hear him. Then the sword began to glow, its substance shifting into a larger, more formidable version of its old shape.

When the process was done, Mata Nui handed the sword back to the amazed Ackar.

The Glatorian hefted it, testing the balance of the weapon, and admiring the quality of the blade. Suddenly, the sword glowed red-hot in his hand. Flames leapt to life along the blade and shot from the tip, scorching a sand dune nearby.

"What in—" Ackar said.

Mata Nui was not surprised. "Of course," he said. "Fire is your elemental power . . . it is the heart of your tribe. The Mask of Life has simply ignited it. You have become a true Toa."

Ackar had no idea what the term meant, but from the way Mata Nui said, it was obviously meant as a compliment. He put his hand on Mata Nui's shoulder and said simply, "Thank you, friend."

Mata Nui looked down at the sand, and then back up at Ackar. "Strange. I have worn many titles, been called many things . . . but never 'friend.'"

Kiina stepped forward, holding her trident out to Mata Nui. "Me next."

Mata Nui took the weapon from her. "I will do what I can for you, but then I must continue my journey. I must find a way to free my people."

"You're not going to help us?" asked Gresh.

"No," said Mata Nui. "I have my own battles to fight."

"Mata Nui, trust me," said Ackar. "I've seen you fight. You're quick, you have some style, but . . . you're not ready. Stay with us a while and I'll teach you everything I know."

Mata Nui considered the proposal. He did not know where his destiny would lead him, and still suspected it was a path he was meant to walk on his own. But this was a world of unknown dangers, and here he had already found a rare treasure: friends who would fight beside him. Having done that, could he really go back to being alone again?

He looked at Ackar, his answer written in his eyes. The veteran Glatorian smiled and clasped Mata Nui's hand.

"Welcome to the team, other-worlder," Kiina said. "Now let's go to work."

Ackar kept his word. As they traveled toward the village of Tesara, he began schooling Mata Nui in the art of combat. The first lesson was not fighting moves, but the power of observation. By studying the subtle movements of a bird in flight, it was possible to predict which direction it would turn. The same could be done in battle to guess an opponent's next move.

As night fell on the second day of their journey, Berix was in the driver's seat of Kiina's chariot, with Gresh riding along beside. Kiina, Ackar, and Mata Nui walked.

"Unfair," said Gresh. "I score this clawed-out new weapon, and Mata Nui tells me I've got awesome 'Toa' powers—whatever those are—but none you will let me test them out."

Kiina smiled. She had been after Gresh for a while to "lighten up." For a young Glatorian, he had always been much too grim and serious. It seemed that he had taken her words to heart.

"You mean like this?" she said, laughing as she thrust her trident forward. Three jets of water shot from the tines of the weapon, striking a pile of boulders and blasting the rocks to bits.

Gresh raised his new shield with his good arm. "Come on . . . just a little test?"

"Patience is the first lesson in becoming a great Glatorian," said Ackar.

"Oh, I think this is pretty great," said Kiina, firing another blast of water from her trident.

Ackar stepped right in front of her water jet, fire sword raised. As the water struck his blade, it turned to steam.

"Guess it's a standoff," said Kiina.

A sudden blast of sand struck the cloud of steam, blowing it away. Kiina and Ackar turned to see Gresh hurling a mini-cyclone from his shield at the ground. The concentrated air was hurling the sand aloft with amazing force.

"Looks like I can blow you both away," Gresh said, smiling.

Kiina's expression brightened. "Better yet—why not combine our powers?"

"Enough," said Ackar. "There's more to winning a fight than fancy weapons. And let me tell you, Mata Nui isn't the only one that could use a few tips. You've got raw talent, Gresh, and a lot of courage, but that will only take you so far. Kiina, I saw your last match with Vastus in Tesara. You let your guard down and he almost took your head off."

Berix burst out laughing. "Ha, Kiina, he got you there!"

Kiina whipped around and smacked Berix out of the driver's seat with her trident. Gresh leaned forward to grab the wheel and keep the vehicle from veering off course. Ackar stepped forward and grabbed the shaft of Kiina's weapon.

"Stop it, both of you. Pay attention and

you might actually learn something—like this!" Ackar said, as he turned on Mata Nui and slashed downward with his fire blade. Mata Nui barely blocked the blow with his own sword, but the impact knocked him backward into Kiina. Click flew from his shoulder and landed on Kiina's arm.

"See?" said Ackar. "You have to learn to read your opponent's next move, before it happens."

Kiina wasn't paying attention. She was eyeing the beetle on her arm warily. "Watch it," she said to Click. "I'm warning you. I'll bite back."

Click opened his pincers as if to snap at her, but before it could do so, Ackar had grabbed it by the shell. The Glatorian lifted the beetle into the air.

"Study your opponent's fighting style," Ackar continued. "Find their weakness, then use it against them . . . if you can."

Click snapped his pincers together angrily. Ackar tossed the insect back to Mata Nui.

The beetle settled contentedly on his shoulder once more.

Dawn brought a return of stifling heat to the desert. The group had been spending the days under whatever shelter they could find, but this morning there was no need to hunt for a cave or a rock outcropping. As they came over a rise, they could see two villages in a large patch of jungle. Great trees dominated the landscape, with vines trailing everywhere. A Glatorian arena sat in the center, separating the villages, but it did not look at all like the one Mata Nui had seen in Vulcanus. This arena was constructed of wood and vines, which formed a latticework roof over the fighting area.

"Where are we?" asked Mata Nui.

"The twin villages of Tesara," said Ackar. "Gresh's home."

The sound of cheering drifted up from the villages. "Sounds like a match is about to start," said Gresh. "Vastus must be fighting today."

"Not if I can help it," said Ackar.

The others looked at him, surprised both by his words and the fierce tone in which he said them. The Vulcanus Glatorian ignored them and started marching toward Tesara. After a moment, the rest of the group followed along behind.

In the arena, Metus sat with Raanu and other Agori in the stands, watching as the Glatorian were announced. The main match for the day pitted the very experienced Vastus of Tesara against the reigning champion of all Glatorian, Tarix of Tajun. Had the great tournament in Atero taken place this year, it was possible Tarix would have been robbed of his title by someone else, most likely a Skrall Glatorian. But the Skrall attack on the arena had brought the tournament to a violent halt, so Tarix remained the official champion.

Following the main match, there would be training matches between some of the newer Glatorian Metus was managing. That had brought Raanu here, in hopes of finding a new fighter for Vulcanus.

Ackar and his team had reached the outskirts of the village by now. Berix lagged behind, glancing uneasily from side to side.

"Why so jumpy, thief?" asked Kiina. "Rip someone off around here? Or just looking for a Skrall to tell our plans to?"

"I'm not a traitor or a thief," Berix answered. Then he added nervously, "But I have done a little . . . collecting . . . around here, so best to lie low." His eyes chanced upon an axe hanging from a nearby doorway and he reached for it, saying, "Oh, I like that. . . ."

Kiina slapped his hand away. "This is not the time, Berix. Got that?"

Metus spotted Ackar, Gresh, and Mata Nui approaching. He rose from his seat, smiling broadly. "What a surprise! Welcome, friends. Isn't this great? A sold-out crowd. I knew pitting Vastus against Tarix would pack them in. Mata Nui, I hope your appearance means you're ready to—"

Ackar cut him off. "It's over."

"Over?" said Raanu, confused. He turned to Metus. "What is he talking about?"

Metus shrugged. "Who knows, with him? He might still be upset about that match with Strakk . . . or maybe he's been out in the sun too long. I'll talk to him."

The fight promoter walked over to Ackar. "Uh, listen, Ackar. With all due respect, you don't have any authority here—this is a match between Tesara and Tajun. And you're too late anyway."

Metus gestured toward the arena. The match had indeed already started. Tarix had fired his Thornax launcher, but Vastus dove aside before the explosive sphere could strike him. It slammed into the ground and went off, sending a spray of shattered rock into the air. He hit the ground and rolled, ending up on his feet and firing his own launcher at Tarix.

The Tajun Glatorian saw the Thornax coming at him, but too late to move aside. He brought his weapon up to block it, but the explosive impact still sent him reeling. Ackar had seen more than enough. He stepped up to the railing, even as Metus tried to block his way. "Wait, what are you doing?" asked Metus, his tone a little frantic. Ackar might have already seen his best days, but Metus knew he was still a Glatorian that others listened to. If he spoke out against the Glatorian system, who knew what might happen?

Gresh, Kiina, and Mata Nui moved to Ackar's side, pushing Metus out of the way. Ackar leaned over the rail, his eyes scanning the crowd of Agori and the two Glatorian fighters.

"Listen to me," Ackar said. "All fighting between Glatorian must stop. Our real enemy is out there, in the desert."

The response of the villagers was shouts of, "Sit down, you fool!" and "Mind your own business!" As serious as Glatorian matches were, they were also one of the few sources of entertainment for Agori. Beings who spent each day just trying to scrape together enough resources to survive needed whatever distraction they could get and weren't in any hurry to give it up.

It was the voice of Tarix that silenced the shouting. "Quiet," said the Glatorian. "Let him talk."

Vastus moved to stand beside Tarix. "I agree. Speak, Ackar."

"Thank you, Vastus. And you, Tarix," Ackar said. "Now listen to me, everyone. The Bone Hunters and the Skrall have formed an alliance."

This provoked a chorus of disbelief from the crowd. Some threw their hands up into the air and turned away. One Agori could be heard saying, "Why are they making us listen to some old loser's fantasies? Get on with the match!"

"It's true," said Kiina. "Tarix . . . our village has been destroyed. I saw it with my own eyes. We arrived too late to help. The Agori who were there escaped, probably out into the sands, but . . . it's gone . . . all of it."

"Impossible . . ." Tarix whispered. "I should have been there. I told Metus this match was a bad idea, especially when you would be in Vulcanus, but Tajun needs the food that was at stake here. And now you say there is no more Tajun."

"Kiina speaks the truth," said Gresh. "Tajun is gone, and it's just the beginning."

"We must unite," said Ackar. "Time is running out."

As soon as he said it, Ackar knew he had made a mistake. The Agori—before simply angry and skeptical—had now become a fearful mob. Who could blame them? Many of them had seen firsthand the aftermath of Bone Hunter raids and the Skrall destruction of Atero. They had witnessed Glatorian running before the might of the Skrall army. Why should they believe Glatorian could save them now that their two worst enemies had joined together?

Raanu chose that moment to step forward.

He held his hands out to the crowd, gesturing for them to sit down and be silent. "Calm yourselves," he said. "Your village leaders will know what is best for you. We will do as we always have."

Mata Nui could no longer to stay quiet. He knew all too well the dangers of underestimating an enemy or expecting that the old methods of dealing with a problem would always work. It was thinking like that which had cost him a universe.

"Your old ways will not work," Mata Nui told the crowd. "You are facing a unified army now. I have seen this before. They will not stop until your people are destroyed."

"This is crazy," said Metus. "It can't be as bad as all that. Maybe . . . maybe the Skrall and the Bone Hunters just happened to hit Tajun at the same time. There might not be any alliance at all. We could be getting all upset over nothing."

"Nothing?" said Tarix, outraged. "You call the destruction of my village nothing? Be glad you are not a Glatorian, Metus, or I would have your head for that."

Raanu turned to Ackar, his voice a harsh whisper. "We have no weapons, Ackar, not any that can stop the Skrall. You know that. How can we fight back?"

"Enough!" yelled Ackar, as he thrust his weapon up into the air. Fire erupted from the blade, lancing high into the morning sky. As one, the crowd gasped and started to back away.

"Yeah, we kinda thought that would get your attention," said Kiina.

"Toa Mata Nui has offered to help us build up our defenses," said Ackar. "With him at our side, I know we can prevail."

Raanu snorted in disbelief. "'Toa' Mata Nui? Why should we trust this stranger?"

The crowd echoed Raanu's sentiments. Mata Nui understood how they felt. After all, he was not one of them. From what he had seen, the Agori lived a hard life. Most likely, trust would not come easily to them, even in the best of circumstances. And this was far from the best of circumstances.

"Tarix, give Mata Nui your weapon," Ackar said.

The Tajun Glatorian stepped forward reluctantly and handed Mata Nui his crude sword. "What is he going to do with it?"

"Show you the power you already possess," said Ackar.

Mata Nui brought Tarix's weapon to his brow. As soon as the weapon touched the Mask of Life, it transformed, becoming a far more ornate and powerful looking sword. Tarix and the Agori looked on, stunned.

"I don't believe it," Tarix said, as Mata Nui handed him his new weapon. "It's . . . incredible."

Ackar turned back to the crowd of villagers. "What more proof do you need? The time to unite the villages has come. If we stand together, we will win."

The Agori burst into cheers, all but Raanu. He still looked unconvinced. Gesturing once more for silence and receiving it, he looked up at Ackar. "If we agree, do you Glatorian and this Mata Nui swear to stay and protect us?"

Kiina, Gresh, Ackar, Tarix, and Vastus nodded their assent. Then all eyes turned to Mata Nui.

"You do not have to ask for the allegiance of the Glatorian. You know where our loyalties lie," Ackar replied to Raanu. Then he turned to Mata Nui. "But we cannot speak for you. I will not pretend I have anything left to teach you. But I'll ask: as friend . . . will you help us?"

Mata Nui reached out and locked arms with Ackar. "Then, as a friend . . . I will stay."

The five Glatorian formed a circle around their new ally. Raising their weapons in the air, filled with the hope of victory, they cried out, "We fight together!"

Their shout echoed across the desert, ringing from the mountains and riding the wind across the dunes. Somewhere, a Bone

Hunter's rock steed cocked its head, wondering at the noise. The beast pawed the ground, every sense alert, eager to charge. For though it could not understand the words the Glatorian had spoken, it knew well the meaning of the tone.

It was a battle cry.

⟩⟨ F I V E ⟩⟨

Ackar knew there was no time to waste. He and the other Glatorian immediately began organizing the defenses of Tesara. With the aid of Mata Nui and the Agori, they erected crude stone walls, mounted Thornax launchers, and dug pit traps in the sand. Kiina worked with the Agori, teaching them how best to use their weapons against mounted foes.

"What makes you so certain the Skrall will strike here next?" Mata Nui asked Ackar as they worked.

"It's the only thing that makes sense," Ackar replied. "As soon as we saw the Bone Hunters are working with them, a lot of things began to make sense."

"Like what?"

"Not long ago, the Bone Hunters started targeting Kiina's village, Tajun," Ackar explained. "Raiding trade caravans, killing Agori, doing everything they could to cut the village off from the rest of Bara Magna. Since Tajun sits on an oasis, you hurt them, you hurt everyone, because they run the water trade."

"That does make sense," Mata Nui agreed.

"After Tajun, what village has the most valuable resource? Iconox, to the north — they have a huge deposit of exsidian, a metal that resists wear even in the worst sandstorms. It's much prized for use in weapons. If the Skrall want to eliminate our ability to fight back, that's the most logical place to strike."

"And Tesara?"

"Lies right between the two villages," said Ackar. "The combined Skrall-Bone Hunter legion hit Tajun, and they'll want Iconox. But they can't afford to leave Tesara sitting behind their lines. They'll be out to destroy it before they move on Iconox."

Mata Nui heard a cheer coming from the

other Glatorian. He turned to see that the walls were complete and the pits concealed.

"Well done," said Tarix. "We did it."

"The Skrall will never know what hit them," said Gresh.

I truly hope not, thought Mata Nui. *But are the Skrall somewhere even now, saying the same thing about us?*

That night was quiet. Kiina stood guard with a group of handpicked Agori, watching for any movement in the desert. The other Glatorian and villagers tried to rest, though sleep proved elusive for most. Bone Hunters were known for making night attacks, often traveling without torches or any other means of illumination. It was frequently the case that by the time a village knew they were coming, it was too late to do anything about it.

Kiina was standing watch on the eastern edge of the village when she heard a sound. It was the barely audible noise of armored feet treading through sand, but it was not coming from beyond Tesara. No, it was from off to her right. Someone was slipping out of the village and into the desert.

The traitor, she said to herself. *Now I've got you.*

She readied her trident and moved off in the direction of the sound. In the pale glow of the village torches, she caught sight of an Agori walking swiftly away from Tesara. Doing her best to stay silent, she followed.

Kiina caught up to the Agori just as he reached the Tesara hot springs. Seizing him from behind, she spun him around. In the moonlight, she could see clearly who it was, and she was not a bit surprised.

"I have to admit, I was hoping I was wrong," Kiina said. "Don't move, traitor."

Berix looked up at her, panic in his eyes. "What? No! You've got it all wrong. I was following—"

A soft voice came from behind the Glatorian. "He was following me."

Berix and Kiina both turned at the sound. "You?!" said Kiina in surprise.

The shadows around them began to move. The next instant, a dozen Skrall and Bone Hunters closed in on them, weapons primed and ready.

". . . And this is how you block a Certavus double-strike," Ackar said, showing off a defensive move it had taken him years to master. Tarix, Vastus, Gresh, and Mata Nui looked on, suitably impressed. Of the lot, only Tarix was agile enough to duplicate the maneuver, and even he doubted he could do it without lots of practice.

The demonstration was interrupted by Metus. "Ackar! Mata Nui!" he shouted. "The Skrall have kidnapped Berix and Kiina!"

"What? How?" said Ackar.

Now Raanu rushed up to the group.

"I saw them, too," he said. "They were being dragged away through the hot springs."

"We must go after them," said Mata Nui," before they get too far. We cannot leave them to the mercies of the Skrall."

"Agreed," said Ackar.

"I'm going with you," said Gresh. "My wound has healed. I'm ready."

By now, the whole village was roused. The Agori crowded around the Glatorian. Some wondered aloud what was going on, while those who knew looked at the Glatorian with worry on their faces.

"No," said Raanu. "You can't leave us. Don't you see, this is just what the Bone Hunters and the Skrall want. They'll lead you away, then wipe us out—just like Tajun."

"He's right," an Agori villager shouted.

"You have to stay!" said another. The cry was picked up by the rest of the crowd, born of panic and unreasoning fear.

"I understand your feelings," Mata Nui said

to the assembled Agori. "But we cannot turn our backs on our friends."

"Kiina is just one Glatorian," Raanu answered. "And Berix is a worthless thief, everyone knows that."

"No one is worth sacrificing, no matter how small," said Mata Nui. "We stand together, as a team."

"So you'd leave us defenseless?" demanded Raanu. "A fine thing! We trusted you with our lives, and you repay us with betrayal."

Mata Nui looked at Ackar and Gresh, then back at Raanu. "I was once forced to abandon my own people. I will not do so again. The Glatorian will remain here. I will go after Berix and Kiina . . . alone."

"No!" said Gresh. "You can't!"

"One being alone, even you, Mata Nui, against a horde of Skrall and Bone Hunters?" said Ackar. "It would be suicide, my friend, and it would help Berix and Kiina not at all."

Mata Nui held up his hand to silence them. "We will see each other again. I promise you." Then he turned and walked out of the village.

"Let me go with him," Gresh said to Ackar. "He doesn't stand a chance alone."

Ackar watched his friend disappear into the darkness. The last glint of moonlight reflected off the shell of Click, perched on its master's shoulder. "He's not alone," the Glatorian said.

Dawn found Ackar climbing a rise toward a great petrified tree stump. Mata Nui sat atop the stump, deep in meditation.

"I thought I might find you up here," said Ackar gently.

Mata Nui smiled. "Thank you, Ackar . . . for everything."

Ackar shook his head. "I should be thanking you. I'd lost faith in others . . . and myself." The Glatorian held a rolled-up piece of parchment out to Mata Nui. "Here. This might help."

Mata Nui spread the parchment out. It was a map of the world of Bara Magna. Ackar pointed to a spot in the northeast, labeled "Roxtus" on the map.

"My guess is they'll be there," said Ackar. "Berix may not be a valuable prisoner, but Kiina is. Of all of us, she's the only one who ever came close to beating a Skrall in the arena. They'll make her the star of one of their matches . . . before they kill her."

Mata Nui could hear what Ackar was leaving unsaid. Kiina meant a lot to the Glatorian. It was tough on him, leaving her safety in the hands of someone else. But the alternative would be rebellion by the Agori—or worse, their surrender to the Skrall.

"I wish I could go with you," said Ackar. "I know, I know . . . you're ready." Pointing down to Tesara, he added, "The question is, are they?"

Mata Nui followed his gaze. Down below, the Agori were laboring to pull their two massive shelters together. Two structures separated by an arena were more vulnerable to a "divide and conquer" Skrall attack. One could be more easily defended.

"Uniting the two halves of Tesara is a start," said Mata Nui.

"Let's hope the rest of the villages survive long enough to join us," Ackar answered.

Ackar suddenly feinted a jab at Mata Nui's face. Mata Nui moved like lightning, bringing his hand up to block Ackar's fist. Ackar burst out laughing.

"You've learned well, my friend," he said, slapping Mata Nui on the back.

"I had a great teacher," Mata Nui replied, smiling.

A great boom suddenly rocked the desert. Mata Nui and Ackar looked down below to see that the Agori had succeeded in uniting the two shelters into one. While both large metal structures had looked impressive before, connected together they were a formidable sight that might make even a Skrall hesitate before invading.

But their new appearance had an even

more profound effect on Mata Nui. His eyes widened slightly and he gasped. Now he knew why the huge shelters had looked so familiar to him. It had been right in front of him all along, but with all that had been going on, he hadn't seen it.

"Incredible. . . ." he whispered.

"What is it?" asked Ackar.

Mata Nui wanted to shout the answer to the skies. It was amazing, wonderful . . . it could be the key to his regaining his lost universe. But now was not the time to reveal what he had learned to Ackar, not when the Glatorian faced such a serious threat. When the Skrall were defeated, there would be time to share his revelation.

"I will explain . . . later," he said, beginning his descent back down the mountain.

Ackar watched him go, wondering what had gotten into his friend. Sure, seeing the shelters coming together was a good start, inspiring, even . . . but hardly "incredible." Well, sometimes there was no figuring out

Mata Nui, he thought, and that was to be expected. He was from a completely different world, after all.

Will he ever make it back home? Ackar asked himself. *I know that's what he wants. But I am not so sure Bara Magna can stand to lose him.*

Roxtus was the largest village in all of Bara Magna, big enough to be called a city. Home to the Skrall warriors and the rock tribe Agori, it was a place few had visited even before the war had begun. The Skrall were not friendly or particularly good hosts. Most of the Glatorian or Agori who wound up there did so against their will, having been captured by Bone Hunters and sold into slavery in Roxtus.

Since the attack on Atero, of course, no one had dared come within miles of Roxtus if they could avoid it. The city was an armed camp, with Skrall troops drilling for a planned campaign and Agori guards talking about how they wished they could be there to watch the other villages fall. Outside the walls, Bone Hunters scoured the desert, watching for Agori spies and Glatorian raiders.

Kiina and Berix were getting a look at life inside Roxtus. Hanging in a cage suspended high in the air, Berix was starting to think they might have been better off buried under the Skopio. It didn't help that Kiina had decided their captivity was all his fault, not to mention that she was still angry about his activities in the Tajun cave.

"It was my cavern," she insisted for the third time. "You should have stayed out of it!"

"Oh, really? *Your* cavern?" snapped Berix. "You stole it! You're a thief, just like me."

"That—no!" said Kiina. "And I thought you said you were a collector, you little weasel!"

"Ah-hah, now she remembers. How things change when the metal claw is on the other foot."

"That doesn't even make sense," Kiina sputtered. "Look, that cavern was my secret place . . . my private sanctuary from all the ugliness outside. . . . Can you understand that?"

Berix looked at the expression in Kiina's eyes and suddenly felt all the anger drain out of him. Bara Magna wasn't the easiest place to live. Probably everyone needed some kind of an escape. For him, it was "collecting;" for Kiina, the cave and her dreams of someday getting off this planet. Most other Glatorian just threw themselves into training nonstop as a way of ignoring the harsh realities of life in the desert.

"Yeah. I can," Berix said, after a long moment. "I've got feelings, too, you know. And by the way, I didn't steal them."

Kiina actually smiled warmly at Berix. He couldn't believe it. "No," she said. "You just collected them."

Berix smiled back. "Didn't you ever think that maybe you weren't the only one who needed to believe that there was something more?"

Kiina didn't reply, just looked away. The silence that followed was uncomfortable. Berix had never seen Kiina so . . . vulnerable before. He had to admit that he was guilty of the same thing as she: He had never bothered to think about her feelings. Maybe if they had stopped shouting at each other for a minute, they might have settled the cave issue between them long ago.

"I've got an idea," he offered. "Maybe we could share the cavern? It could be our secret place. I mean, once the Glatorian rescue us. . . . Um, they are going to rescue us, aren't they?"

Kiina gestured at the fortress in which they were held prisoner, bristling as it was with armed Skrall and Agori. "Look where we are, Berix. I wouldn't count on it."

Berix's smile disappeared. Then suddenly it was back, twice as bright as before. "Yeah, well, then what's that?" he said, pointing toward the gate.

Kiina looked down. Mata Nui, shield in

hand, was walking into the city of Roxtus. Mounted Bone Hunters rode behind him, prodding him towards the central arena. But this was no prisoner they were escorting, that was obvious. His head was held high.

Hearing the commotion, Tuma, leader of the Skrall, stepped out of his shelter and walked to the center of the arena. He stood still, sizing Mata Nui up as the hero approached. Tuma had heard stories about this one from the Bone Hunters who survived the Skopio fight. He had been prepared to credit this new Glatorian with skill and daring, but obviously the warrior was lacking in sense if he walked into Roxtus alone.

This stranger will learn a lesson, thought Tuma, *and a painful one. He walked into my city—he will not be walking out again.*

⊃⊂ S I X ⊃⊂

"I don't believe it," said Kiina. Her thoughts were a jumble. There was excitement, relief, and surprise that someone had actually come to their rescue. There was puzzlement—where were Ackar, Gresh, Tarix, and the others? Why had Mata Nui come alone? And there was fear, too. She knew what Mata Nui had let himself in to do, and she worried about what might happen to him in this nest of sand snakes.

"Neither does Tuma," Berix replied.

That might have been true, but if it was, Tuma was careful not to show it. The Skrall chief radiated power and confidence as Mata Nui approached. "I'd hoped all the Glatorian would come," he said. "But it seems they are even bigger cowards than I thought."

Mata Nui ignored the jibe. He marched up the ramp that led into the arena, paying no attention to the chained Vorox on either side of it who tried to claw at him, or the laughter of nearby Skrall warriors. Tuma reminded him of someone else he had known, in his past, so full of belief in his own might. Beings like Tuma, he knew, drew their power from the fear they provoked in those around them. Confronted by someone who felt no such fear, they often crumbled.

In the cage, Berix gave a little wave to Mata Nui as he passed underneath. "Is he —?" he began.

"Alone," Kiina finished for him. "I'm not sure I want to look."

Tuma turned to look at the crowd of Skrall and Agori. Gesturing toward Mata Nui, he said, "Either he's a madman or he wants to join the winning side." He turned to look at Mata Nui, an evil grin plastered on his features. "Which is it?"

Mata Nui walked right up to Tuma. The Skrall leader towered over him, but Mata Nui was not intimidated. He looked Tuma in the eyes and said, "I am here to fight for my friends' freedom, one-on-one. Unless the leader of the Skrall is the true coward?"

Anger flashed in Tuma's eyes, but his tone of voice stayed amused, even a little bored. "I'm going to enjoy tearing that fancy mask from your face."

Before Mata Nui could reply, Tuma lashed out, landing a solid blow and sending his opponent sprawling in the sand. The Skrall and Bone Hunters cheered wildly. This was going to be a good fight, if a short one.

"Hey! No fair!" yelled Berix.

"Dirty, cheating Skrall," Kiina said.

Tuma wasn't letting up. He brought his huge sword down hard on Mata Nui's shield. Mata Nui rolled away and got to his feet, but Tuma was on him in an instant. The Skrall leader struck again and again, battering Mata Nui around the arena at will. Tuma was enjoying this, but some part of him wondered—could it be this easy? Why wasn't this Glatorian fighting back?

Above, Berix covered his eyes with his hands. "Oh, I can't watch. Mata Nui's getting shredded."

"No, no, don't you see?" said Kiina. "Watch. He's doing what Ackar taught us—study your opponent, find his weakness."

"Well, he'd better find it fast!" Berix replied.

In the arena, Tuma was feeling more confident than ever of victory. He wasn't even bothering to keep his shield up anymore. This Glatorian was broken, too much of a coward to even raise his sword in defense. He was certainly far from being a worthy opponent for the leader of the warrior Skrall, but perhaps he could be a chew toy for the Vorox after Tuma was done with him.

"Did this pathetic weakling really believe

he could bring down the mighty Tuma?" the Skrall leader bellowed to the crowd.

"Be careful," said Mata Nui. "Arrogance can topple giants. Trust me . . . I know."

Tuma had grown tired of this sport. It was time to end it. He swung his sword in what would surely be the killing blow.

But the strike did not connect. Mata Nui moved so fast he was almost a blur, ducking under the sword and slipping past his attacker. As Tuma's momentum carried the Skrall leader forward, Mata Nui helped his opponent along with a sharp elbow to the back. Tuma grunted and staggered a few steps.

The Skrall leader turned on Mata Nui, enraged. He swung his sword wildly, but where his blows had never missed before, now hitting Mata Nui was like trying to strike a desert wind. Mata Nui ducked and dodged each blow, then took advantage of his opponent's being off-balance to land solid shots of his own. Each one rocked Tuma a little more, causing the Skrall chief to slow down just a bit. Faster and more agile, Mata Nui took full advantage of his foe's fatigue, striking and then backing away before Tuma's sword could hit.

In the cage, Kiina was so excited she was shaking Berix. "That's it! Tuma's huge, but he's slow. Mata Nui's using the Skrall's own strength as leverage against him."

"I get it! I get it!" Berix said, feeling like she was going to rattle his brains loose in a second.

The tide of battle had turned, and even Tuma knew it. With each blow Mata Nui evaded, his fury and his carelessness grew. "I'll crush you like an insect!" he raged.

Remembering the origins of his shield, Mata Nui smiled. "Don't be so fast to knock insects, Tuma. Sure, they're small—but their sting can fell a giant, wouldn't you agree?"

Tuma swung at Mata Nui's head and missed once more; Mata Nui ducked inside his guard to strike two more hard blows. Tuma was exhausted and reeling. Mata Nui knew it was time to finish this fight.

Summoning all his remaining strength, Mata Nui brought his blade down in a final sweeping blow, shattering Tuma's weapon to bits. Without pausing, Mata Nui spun, lashing out with a kick that sent Tuma crashing to his knees. Tuma looked up at Mata Nui, his body teetering for a moment. Then the Skrall leader collapsed into the sand.

All around, the Skrall, Bone Hunters, and Agori gasped in shock. Mata Nui ignored them, instead reaching down to pick up the fallen Tuma's shield. Raising it high over his head, he proclaimed, "I claim Tuma's shield in victory! Release my friends."

In the cage above, Berix and Kiina embraced in wild celebration. "He did it!" shouted Berix.

"He really did it! Woo-hoo!" cried Kiina.

Silence reigned in the Skrall arena now. Tuma was conscious, but too weak to rise. The Skrall, amazingly, had not charged Mata

Nui, perhaps too in shock that their leader had fallen. Mata Nui still held the shield aloft, waiting for his foes to honor the deal he had made with their leader.

Then there came the strange sound of one pair of hands clapping and all too familiar laughter. Mata Nui turned to see Metus standing at the entrance to the arena, Kiina's trident in his hand. All around, the Skrall drew their weapons.

"I could always pick a winner. Now throw down your shield and your sword," said Metus. When Mata Nui did not respond, Metus' smile abruptly disappeared. "That's not a joke."

Mata Nui tossed his blade onto the sand and then gently laid down his shield. There was a flash of light as the shield transformed back into Click. "Save yourself," Mata Nui whispered to the insect. The beetle gave a quick click of its mandibles and then vanished underground.

Metus hurled Kiina's trident at the spot where the scarabax had vanished, but too late. The head of the trident stabbed into the sand, leaving the weapon sticking out of the ground.

"So you were the traitor all along," said Mata Nui coldly.

"Coward!" Kiina screamed from above. "Keeping tabs on the Glatorian so you could sell us out to the Bone Hunters."

"Not a coward," Metus said, smiling. "Just a good businessman."

"You were the one who convinced the Skrall and the Bone Hunters to unite," said Mata Nui.

Metus gestured to the assembled army of Skrall warriors and nomadic bandits. "Of course I did. You think they'd come up with that idea on their own? As rival tribes, they did little damage, always having to be watchful of each other, but together...under one ruler..."

Kiina couldn't believe what she was hearing. "You'd lead them against your own people?"

Metus spat on the ground. "What have the Agori ever done for me?"

"Uh, let's see," said Berix. "We trusted you?"

"The Glatorian will tear you apart for this," Kiina said through gritted teeth.

Metus glanced at Kiina, then back to Mata Nui. "She still doesn't understand."

"We are the only ones that know your role in this," agreed Mata Nui. "The other Glatorian still see you as an ally."

"Exactly," said Metus. "And by the time the Glatorian realize it, the battle will already be over. I win."

Metus turned to his army. "Finish them! I've wasted enough time here; I have to get back to—"

His orders were interrupted by the sound of Bone Hunters grunting in alarm. The nomads were pointing toward the desert, their bodies actually shaking with fear. Metus turned and immediately saw why—there was a Glatorian heading for the city. But not just any Glatorian; no, this one shimmered in the sunlight and was easily 100 feet high.

That sight was more than enough for the Bone Hunters, who broke ranks and raced away in terror. Some didn't even pause to mount their rock steeds, just took off into the desert on foot.

"Where are you going?" screamed Metus. "Don't run, you idiots, fight!"

The traitorous Agori pointed at the Vorox, still chained near the entrance to the arena. "Unleash these wretched beasts. Make them fight. If that giant crushes them, so be it!"

Roused from their shock, the Skrall moved to carry out his orders. Loading their Thornax launchers, they prepared for battle with the giant attacker.

Mata Nui took advantage of his captors' distraction. Grabbing both his sword and Kiina's trident, he moved swiftly to the chain that held the cage in the air. With one swift stroke, he shattered the chain, sending the cage crashing down into the sand. The impact shattered the prison, freeing Berix and Kiina.

Mata Nui rushed to join them. "Are you all right?" he asked Kiina, handing her the trident.

"I am now that I've got this back," Kiina answered. "Thanks."

Berix didn't share her relief at escaping. His attention was focused on the giant Glatorian who was still marching toward Roxtus. "What *is* that?"

Mata Nui glanced at the giant. In the distance, he could hear a familiar sound—the clicking of a scarabax beetle, multiplied millions of times. He smiled. "I believe, Berix, we are witnessing the true power of unity."

The clicking could be heard by everyone now, so loud it drowned out every other sound. Before the startled eyes of the Skrall, the Glatorian dissolved into a swarm of scarabax beetles. With the giant construct gone, it was now possible to see what had been behind it all along.

"And loyalty . . ." said Mata Nui.

They emerged from the center of a sandstorm like avenging desert spirits. Tarix, Vastus, Ackar, Gresh, and so many more. Glatorian and Agori of every tribe united into one great army. Some were on foot, others in dune chariots and other vehicles. Their weapons ranged from Thornax launchers to rocks and clubs. It was a ragtag force, undisciplined, wild, maybe even suicidal, to dare challenge the Skrall—and it was the most beautiful sight Mata Nui had ever seen.

The Glatorian-led army swept into the city, clashing with the defending Skrall in fierce combat. Atop a wall, Mata Nui, Kiina, and Berix saw the battle begin. Mata Nui handed Tuma's shield to Berix. "Here. You may need this."

"Really?" Berix answered, grinning. "Wow, nobody ever actually *gave* me something before. Can I . . . keep it?"

"Only if you survive," said Kiina. Seeing the worried expression on the Agori's face, she smiled. "Don't worry. Just stay close to me. But hold up—aren't we missing part of the team?"

As if in answer, Click leapt from the sand, landing on the tip of Kiina's trident. Mata Nui reached out as the beetle vanished in a flash of light, transforming back into his shield. Mata Nui's eyes met the single eye in the center of the shield.

"Now we're ready," said Mata Nui.

Mata Nui and Kiina jumped from the wall, Berix following right after. "Wait for me!" the Agori shouted.

Two Skrall mounted on Bone Hunter rock steeds spotted Kiina and Mata Nui leaping down toward them. Before they could fire their Thornax launchers, they had been unseated by a combined attack. Berix, sailing through the air behind them, landed backward on the back of one of the steeds. It immediately took off in a gallop, with Berix hanging on for dear life.

The Agori glanced over his shoulder and saw he was headed right for a Skrall. "Oh, what the heck," Berix said, closing his eyes tightly and swinging his shield downward. "No trial—"

The shield bashed the Skrall on the head, staggering him.

"— no treasure!" Berix smiled, already looking for another target.

Nearby, Mata Nui was in trouble. A mounted Skrall had him pinned down with Thornax launcher blasts. He had managed to dodge them so far, but he was running out of room to maneuver. His shield would protect him for a while, but enough direct hits would shatter it. He needed help.

It came from an unexpected source— Gresh, tearing across the sand, riding his shield down the dunes. As Mata Nui watched, Gresh launched himself into the air, flipped, and slammed shield-first into the Skrall. The impact knocked the Thornax launcher out of the Skrall's hand. Mata Nui charged, stabbed his sword into the ground, and used it to vault himself into the air and snag the launcher.

As he fell toward the ground, Mata Nui saw the image of an attacking Skrall reflected in the metal surface of the launcher. He landed on his feet, whirled, and smashed his shield into the Skrall. As the warrior went down, Mata Nui saw Kiina with a mounted Skrall riding after her. He tossed her the Thornax launcher. She caught it and fired in one smooth motion, blasting the ground in front of the rock steed. Animal and rider flew into the air and landed with a heavy thud.

Still, the element of surprise could only work against the Skrall for so long. These were trained and disciplined warriors. Regrouping, they surrounded the Glatorian and pressed in. Mata Nui, Ackar, Gresh, and Kiina found themselves fighting back to back, with their comrades in the same situation not far away.

"They have us outnumbered ten to one," said Ackar, fending off multiple attacks at once.

"More like twenty!" said Kiina.

"Yeah," Gresh added, "but who's counting?"

"Let it be a hundred," said Mata Nui. "We have the true power. We fight with honor and purpose."

Mata Nui brought his sword down against a Skrall shield with such force that the shield exploded into fragments. "For unity!" Mata Nui cried.

"For unity!" the Glatorian echoed, surging forward.

Mata Nui battered two Skrall aside, opening the first gap in the enemy lines. Through it, he saw Metus trying to run.

"So the coward flees. . . ." Mata Nui muttered to himself. He charged toward Metus, who was climbing into his dune chariot accompanied by two Skrall warriors.

Spotting Mata Nui, Metus shouted to his guards, "Well, what are you waiting for? Destroy him!"

But there was no stopping Mata Nui this day. Mata Nui slammed into the two Skrall, knocking them off their feet. With each blow, he thought of his lost universe and people. He remembered the evil that held them captive . . . the same kind of thoughtless cruelty and arrogance that lived in Metus. In his own way, the traitorous Agori was just as bad as the darkness that had overtaken Mata Nui's universe. The Agori wanted power, and he didn't care who had to suffer for it.

Right now, though, all Metus wanted was to put some distance between himself and this battle. He fired up the dune chariot and was about to ride out of the city when he saw two Vorox blocking the way. "Out of my way, you filthy—"

The Vorox grabbed the dune chariot and tipped it over, dumping Metus out onto the sand. Before he could get up again, Mata Nui was upon him, yanking him into the air.

"Wait," pleaded Metus. "We can make a deal. I'll give you whatever you want!"

Mata Nui lifted Metus higher, so the two were at eye level. "I have what I want. You."

The Mask of Life Mata Nui wore began to glow. He brought Metus closer, until the Agori's helmet touched the mask.

"Stop! What are you doing??" screamed Metus.

There was a blinding flash of light. When it dissipated, the Agori was gone, replaced by a hissing serpent with the face of Metus. The mask had done its work well, Mata Nui decided — justice had been done.

"Now everyone will see you for what you truly are," Mata Nui said to the Metus serpent.

Behind him, the Skrall were closing in on Ackar, Kiina, and Gresh. "There's too many!" shouted Kiina over the din of battle.

"We can't fight them all!" said Gresh.

"Our weapons!" said Ackar. "Quick! Combine their power!"

The three Glatorian stood side by side, their sword, trident, and shield touching. A blast erupted from the combined weapons, air, fire, and water together in one devastating force. It blew the Skrall back, but they charged again.

"They're still coming!" said Gresh.

Mata Nui vaulted over the Skrall to land beside his allies. He touched his sword to their weapons. "Now — as one!" he said.

Once more, they fired, this time with the power of life itself added to their energies. The explosive blast flattened the Skrall attackers. Those few who still remained on their feet fled at the sight of so much raw power unleashed. On vehicles, on foot, and on rock steeds, they deserted Roxtus, leaving the Glatorian and Agori the victors.

"We did it!" yelled Gresh.

Mata Nui looked into the eye on his shield. "Thank you," he said.

There was a bright flash of light, and then the shield was gone and Click was sitting on Mata Nui's shoulder once more. Ackar looked at the insect and smiled.

"And I used to think scarabax were just annoying little pests," Ackar said.

The beetle responded with rapid clicks of its mandibles. Ackar laughed at the sight, saying, "Click, I will never doubt you again."

"I can't believe it's over," said Vastus.

"And that all of us are still in one piece," added Tarix.

"Wait," said Kiina, looking around. "Where's Berix?"

"I haven't seen the little guy," said Gresh.

Kiina was frantic now. "I *told* him to stick close to me."

"Kiina—" Ackar said, resting a hand on her shoulder.

"No!" said Kiina. "He was my responsibility. Berix!"

A muffled voice cried out in response. "Down here!"

The Glatorian glanced to the right. Berix's hand was sticking up out of a pile of rubble. "Little . . . help . . . here . . . please!" the Agori said.

Kiina rushed over, grabbed his hand, and yanked Berix free. "You jerk! I thought—" Then she paused and hugged the Agori tight to her chest. "Don't ever do that again."

Berix gasped for air in her too-tight embrace. "You know, I think I liked it better when you hated me."

⟨⟩ EPILOGUE ⟨⟩

Weeks later . . .

Mata Nui stood alone on a rocky peak, staring off into the desert. From far below came the sound of Agori hard at work, but there was another noise mixed in, the sound of celebration. While the Bone Hunters were still active in the wastelands, the Skrall had vanished completely. Perhaps they had gone back north, no one could be sure. What mattered was that their threat had ended. Metus, too, had not been seen since the battle. The unspoken assumption was that he had fallen prey to a sand bat or some other desert predator. No one was shedding any tears over him.

Ackar climbed up to join Mata Nui. He had been busy these last few days overseeing a massive project: the linking together of all the villages of Bara Magna into one mega-city.

"Don't like parties?" he asked, smiling. "Agori from all over Bara Magna are pulling together . . . literally . . . uniting all the villages. And we have you to thank for that."

"No, I was only one piece," Mata Nui replied. "It took each of us to complete the whole. This celebration belongs to the Agori and you—the first leader of the new united villages."

Mata Nui looked down. Using chains, Spikit, and dune chariots, the Agori of Iconox, Vulcanus, and Tajun had dragged their massive shelters across the desert to link up with Tesara. Others had gone north and brought down the huge structure that dominated Roxtus. It had been a mammoth undertaking, and now it was almost finished.

Kiina, Gresh, and Berix came up to join the two friends. "So what now, Mata Nui?" asked the Agori.

"Continue searching for answers," Mata Nui replied, "wherever they may take me."

"Look!" Kiina said. "They've done it!"

With a final, thunderous boom, the last shelter was fitted into place. When the sand and dust finally cleared, the group of heroes got their first look at the newly assembled structure. It was a sight that shocked them all.

"Whoa," said Berix. "Are you seeing what I'm seeing?"

Whatever they had expected, it had not been this. Only Mata Nui had even an inkling of what was to come, and he hadn't dared to hope. But there it was, for all to see—when the shelters were put together, they were revealed to be not just random giant pieces of metal, but pieces of a mechanical being. Once assembled, the head, arms, torso, and legs could each be clearly seen. And the group around Mata Nui could all recall where they had seen such a thing before.

"The giant," said Ackar. "From Kiina's cavern in Tajun . . ."

"How is this possible?" said Gresh. "All this time, we have been living inside pieces of a giant mechanical . . . something?"

"Wait!" said Berix, digging into his pouch. "I've got something. Hold on, where is it . . . here!" He handed Mata Nui an old coin. Inscribed on one side was the figure of a mechanical being, the same figure that was on the wall of the Tajun cavern.

"I collected it from the cave a long time ago," said Berix. "Forgot all about it until I saw that thing down there."

"The two images match," said Ackar.

"Uh-huh," said Berix. "And wait till you see the other side."

Berix flipped the coin over. On the other side was another design, this one matching the mazelike pattern of the Skrall shield Berix still carried.

"Same symbol," said Kiina.

"No, not a symbol," Mata Nui answered. "A map!"

"To where?" asked Gresh.

"That is what I must find out," said Mata Nui, taking the coin from Berix. "That is where my destiny is waiting . . . I know it."

"Don't you mean *we* must find out?" asked Kiina. "Remember your promise to me."

Mata Nui gave a gentle smile. "You are welcome to join me. But I have no idea how long this journey might take, or the dangers that await."

"Do you think that you and that . . . giant . . . are connected somehow?" asked Ackar.

Mata Nui knew the answer, of course. But telling Ackar he had once inhabited the body of a 40-million-foot tall robotic being, a larger version of the one down below, would start a conversation he did not feel like having right now. So all he said was, "Perhaps. But you are looking at an empty shell, the remains of what might have been a great ruler, the guardian of his people."

He paused. It was difficult to get the words out, with so many new emotions swirling inside of him. When Mata Nui finally continued, he said, "Thanks to all of you, I am closer to becoming the warrior I must be if I am to reclaim my empire and free my people."

"This time, though, you won't need to face the fight alone," said Ackar.

Mata Nui smiled. "Then, my friends, our quest begins."

This would be but the first of the adventures Mata Nui would have on Bara Magna. Accompanied by Kiina, Gresh, Ackar, and Berix, he would journey north, past Roxtus, to the lands from which the Skrall had come. Berix would add "chronicler" to his list of hobbies, keeping a record of where they went and what they encountered.

The revelation that a second robot body existed—no doubt a prototype of Mata Nui's own former shell, from some past era—opened a whole new array of mysteries. Had the Great Beings, Mata Nui's creators, actually lived on Bara Magna? And if so, were they here still? Was there a way to find the energy that would power that body, and could Mata Nui's mind inhabit it? And if that was possible, could he take the Agori's shelters away from them in that way, so soon after convincing them to create one great city from the pieces?

There were many questions, and few answers, as the heroes began their journey north. Gresh could guide them a part of the way, as he knew the Black Spikes from an earlier journey, but beyond that it was unexplored territory. The landscapes were wondrous and frightening, the enemies—including the shapeshifters that had plagued the Skrall—fierce and devastatingly destructive. And, as always seemed to be the case, the solution of each mystery seemed to create a dozen more puzzles.

Despite all this, Mata Nui found he was at peace. Once, he had been the ruler of an entire universe, powerful beyond all measure—and yet, he had been alone. Now, though not as strong and the ruler of only his own heart, he had friends beside him. Long ago, he had tried to teach his people about the virtues of unity and duty, but had never truly understood them himself. His time on Bara Magna had taught him much, far more than he had ever taught the Agori and Glatorian.

His destiny still lay before him, even though there might be no chronicler to tell its tale. One day, he would return to do battle for his universe and his people. When that struggle came, he might well be fighting alone again. But he would carry into that challenge the memories of Ackar's bravery, Kiina's resourcefulness, Gresh's daring, and the courage of every Agori. He would fight not only to make up for past failures, but to honor those who chose to stand beside him in his time of trial.

It had been a long journey, and someday others might think it had all been just a legend . . . but for those who had lived the tale, the heroes, the villains, the tragedies, and the triumphs would never be forgotten.